For Mom and Dad.

Thanks for introducing me to Jesus,
believing I can do the impossible,
and helping me achieve my wildest dreams.

This book is as much yours as it is mine.

I love you more!

"Tell the people of Jerusalem, 'Look, your King is coming to you.
He is humble, riding on a donkey—riding on a donkey's colt.'"
~Matthew 21:5 NLT

Howie's Broken Hee-Haw
Copyright © 2022 by Josie Siler
All rights reserved.

End Game Press books may be purchased in bulk at special discounts for sales promotion, corporate gifts, ministry, fund-raising, or educational purposes. Special editions can also be created to specifications. For details, contact Special Sales Dept., End Game Press, P.O. Box 206, Nesbit, MS 38651 or info@endgamepress.com.

Visit our website at www.endgamepress.com.

Scripture quotations are taken from the Holy Bible, New Living Translation, copyright ©1996, 2004, 2015 by Tyndale House Foundation. Used by permission of Tyndale House Publishers, Carol Stream, Illinois 60188. All rights reserved.

Library of Congress Control Number: 2021949343
ISBN: 978-1-63797-011-9
eBook ISBN: 978-1-63797-012-6

Cover & interior design by Monica Thomas for TLC Book Design, TLCBookDesign.com
Illustrated by Sebastien Braun

Printed in India
10 9 8 7 6 5 4 3 2 1

HOWIE'S BROKEN HEE-HAW

By
JOSIE SILER

Illustrated by
SEBASTIEN BRAUN

Little Howie stomped his hooves
in anger. He'd never be able
to Hee-Haw, Hee-Haw
like the other colts.

His second Hee-Haws always turned into
Hee-Ha-La-La-Lay-Lu-Yas.

Howie practiced every day,
but he just couldn't get it right.

He felt like he didn't have
control of his own mouth,
and that made him mad!

Hee-
Haw

Hee-
Ha
La-La-Lay-Lu-Ya

Hee-
Haw

Hee-
Ha
La-La-Lay-Lu-Ya

"Mama! My Hee-Hawer
is still broken!"

"That's enough practice
for today, Howie.
It's your bedtime." Mama said
with a kiss to his head.

"You can try again tomorrow.
Sleep sweet, my dear, and remember
I love you very much."

Howie didn't want to go to bed,
but he had to admit he was sleepy.
All that practice tired him out.
With a big sigh, he curled up in the hay.
Giant tears rolled down his furry snout.

He snuggled deeper into the hay,
drying his tears and telling himself
tomorrow would be a better day.

"I'm not sure, but these men
have come to take us somewhere.
Hurry up, now, they're waiting."

Howie stayed close to his mama as they walked and walked.

Hee-Haw,
Hee-Ha-La-La-Lay-Lu-Yaaaa!
Howie whispered his
broken Hee-Haw.

He wanted to practice, but he didn't
want the men to hear him.

"Well, well, well, who do we have here?"
a kind man asked.

"Hello, sir. My name is Howie."

"Hello, Howie. My name is Jesus,
and I need your help."

"You need my help?" Howie asked.

"How can I help YOU? I'm just a donkey
with a broken Hee-Hawer.
There's lots of donkeys who can help
you better than I can."

"Oh little one, you're not broken.
You're perfect just the way you are."

"I am?"

"You sure are. I chose you to ride
into Jerusalem because I have need
of your special Hee-Haw."

"Jesus," Howie whispered. "I don't know
if I can do it. What if everyone laughs
at my funny Hee-Hawer? I'm scared."

Jesus wrapped his arms around Howie
and whispered in his ear.

"Howie, what did that man say to you?"

"Mama, that man's name is Jesus.
He told me that He needs me!"

"I'm going to carry Him into Jerusalem and he didn't care at all that my Hee-Hawer is broken. He said my Hee-Haw, Hee-Ha-La-La-Lay-Lu-Ya is special and that I was made to praise Him."

And that's just what he did.

Howie carried Jesus down the dusty road toward Jerusalem. As they neared the city Howie saw crowds of people coming out to meet them, and his legs began to shake.

Jesus scratched Howie's ears and said,
"Don't be afraid, little one. Now's the
time to use your special bray."

With that, Howie bellowed the
loudest Hee-Haw, Hee-Ha-La-La-Lay-Lu-Ya
he could muster.

Hee-Ha-
La-La-Lay-
Luuuuu-Ya

Howie's beautiful
Hee-Haw, Hee-Ha-La-La-Lay-Lu-Yas
were heard above the crowds of
people surrounding Jesus.

They laughed in delight at Howie's song of praise and added their own cries of Hosanna in the highest! as Howie and Jesus passed their way.

Joy filled Howie's heart because he knew he was made on purpose, for a purpose.

Prayer

God, I'm so happy that You love me.
It's amazing to think that there is no one else
in the world exactly the same as me.
I'm one of a kind!

I know that You don't make mistakes and
that You made me for a very special reason.
I want to be brave like Howie and use the
special talents that You gave me.

I know You will help me.
Thank You!

Amen.